ISLINGTON LIBRARIES
3 0120 02025877 8
FJ

D0549386

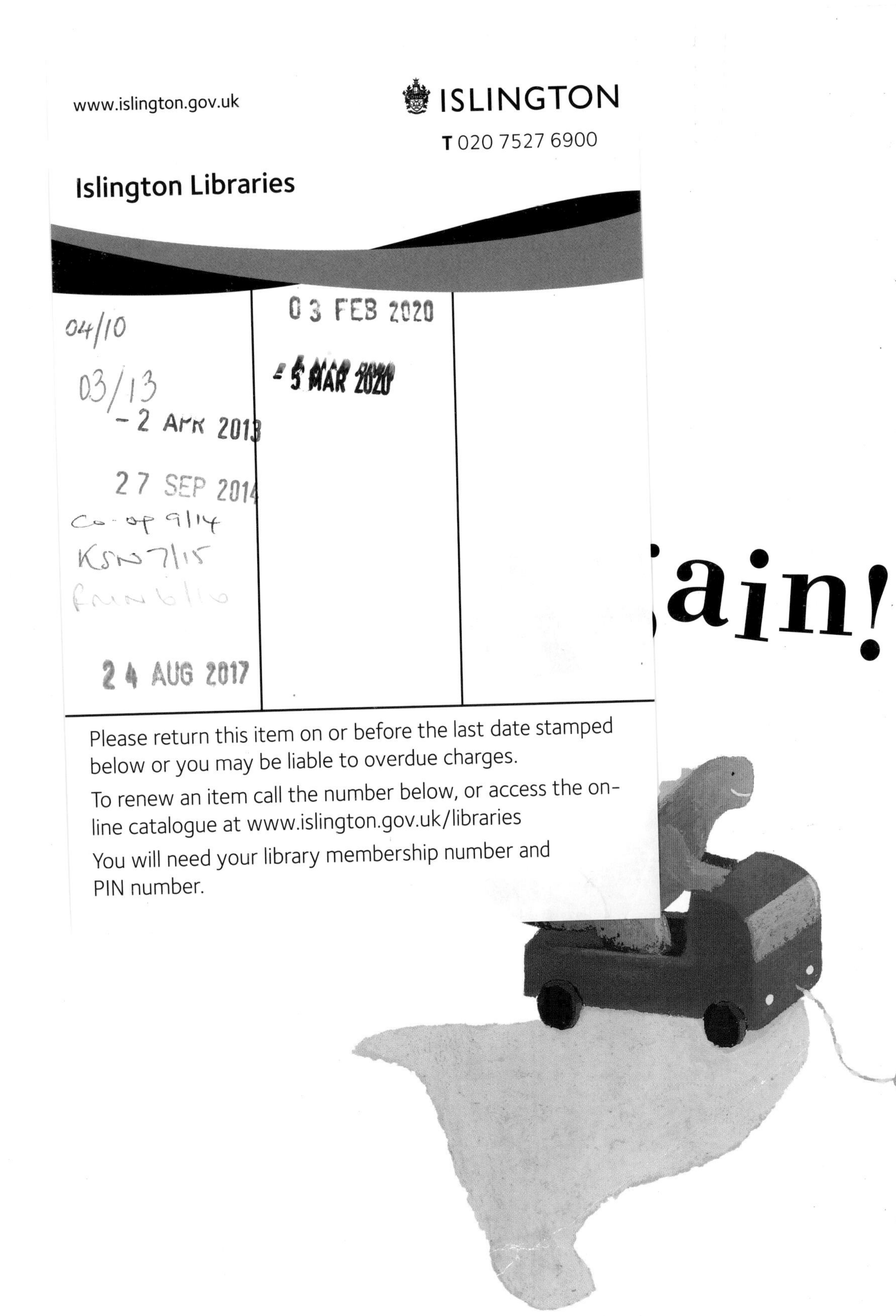
www.islington.gov.uk
ISLINGTON
T 020 7527 6900
Islington Libraries

04/10
03/13
- 2 APR 2013
27 SEP 2014
Co-op 9/14
KSN 7/15
24 AUG 2017
03 FEB 2020
5 MAR 2020

Please return this item on or before the last date stamped below or you may be liable to overdue charges.
To renew an item call the number below, or access the on-line catalogue at www.islington.gov.uk/libraries
You will need your library membership number and PIN number.

ain!

For Ella Rose Kennedy and
Teddy Traynor . . . again – I.W.

For Catherine and Oscar – S.B.

ORCHARD BOOKS
96 Leonard Street, London EC2A 4XD
Hachette Children's Books
Level 17/207 Kent Street, Sydney, NSW 2000
ISBN 1 84362 545 8
First published in Great Britain in 2004
First published in paperback in 2005
Text © Ian Whybrow 2004
Illustrations © Sebastien Braun 2004
The rights of Ian Whybrow to be identified as the author
and Sebastien Braun to be identified as the illustrator
of this work have been asserted by them in accordance
with the Copyright, Designs and Patents Act, 1988.
A CIP catalogue for this book is available from the British Library.
10 9 8 7 6 5 4 3 2 1
Printed in Singapore

Again!

Written by Ian Whybrow

Illustrated by Sebastien Braun

ISLINGTON LIBRARIES
30120020258778
PETERS 06-Feb-06
£5.99 FJ
F

In a ferny part of the forest –
When the moon is shining clear –
With a pile of their favourite bedtime books,
Sit Daddy and Little Brown Bear.

His friend, Fuzz, is up in the branches,
With bees swarming all round his head.
Fuzz says to the bees, "Stop buzzing me, please!
Come down and hear stories instead."

The first book is ever so funny—
The funniest story for years!
Fuzz laughs till he falls over backwards,
And he's runny with honey and tears.

Up from his dam swims the beaver.
He shakes out the water like rain.
He pricks up his ears,
and hears two little bears shout out . . .

". . . Again!
Again!"

Then Daddy Bear reads the story
Of the great big dinosaur.
So Beaver and Fuzz go

stamp, stamp, stamp!

And Little Brown Bear goes . . .

". . . ROAR!"

"Again! Again!"
call the listeners.

"Again! Again!"
they shout.

From a heap of leaves,
Old Porcupine heaves,
He says, "What's all this about?"

The next book
is all about building,
With a big red truck
and crane.
The animals do the

**brrm,
brrm, brrm!**

Then they all shout out,

"Again!"

Far into the night –
To share the delight –

come Squirrel

and Skunk,

Armadillo,

and Bat.

Wolf Cub

Owl

Chipmunk,

and Wildcat.

In the sad parts,
they all blow their noses.

When the train comes, they all do the train.

When it's scary, they shout,

"He's behind you!

Look Out!"

When it's over, they want it,

"Again!"

Then Mummy calls, "Bedtime for Little Brown Bear!"

She carries him up to his cot.
"Did you like reading
with Daddy?" she asks.

And Little Bear
whispers, "A lot!"

"Again."
"Again."
"Again."
"Again."

Soon all the animals fall asleep.
The forest is quiet – but then –
As they dream of those bedtime stories,
They smile and they murmur,

"Again."

"Again."

"Again."

"Again."

The
E
n
d